# Yummy
# Scrummy

**ReadZone Books Limited**

First published in this edition 2015

© in this edition ReadZone Books Limited 2015
© in text Paul Harrison 2005
© in illustrations Belinda Worsley 2005

Paul Harrison has asserted his right under the Copyright Designs
and Patents Act 1988 to be identified as the author of this work.

Belinda Worsley has asserted her right under the Copyright Designs
and Patents Act 1988 to be identified as the illustrator of this work.

Every attempt has been made by the Publisher to secure appropriate
permissions for material reproduced in this book. If there has been any
oversight we will be happy to rectify the situation in future editions or
reprints. Written submissions should be made to the Publisher.

British Library Cataloguing in Publication Data (CIP) is available
for this title.

Printed in Malta by Melita Press.

ISBN 978 1 78322 467 8

**Visit our website: www.readzonebooks.com**

# Yummy Scrummy

Paul Harrison
and Belinda Worsley

"I'm hungry," said Fly.

"Mmm, pizza.
Yummy scrummy."

"Mmm, chips.
Yummy scrummy."

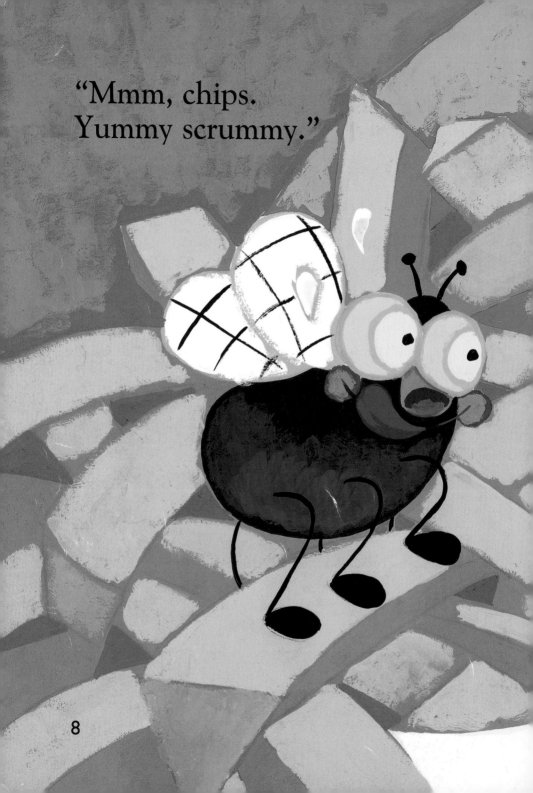

9

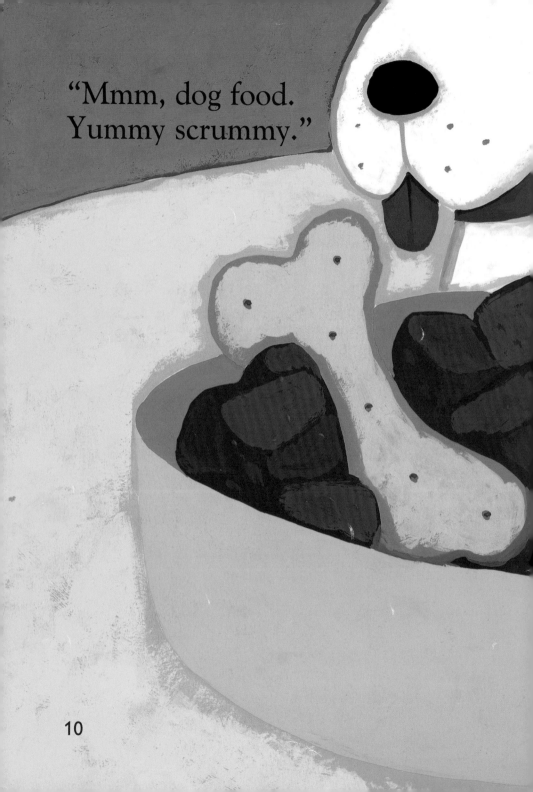

"Mmm, dog food.
Yummy scrummy."

"Mmm, crisps.
Yummy scrummy."

13

"Mmm, cola.
Yummy scrummy."

14

# BURP!

"Time for pudding!"

18

"Mmm, trifle.
Yummy scrummy."

20

"Mmm, chocolate.
Yummy scrummy."

"Mmm, doughnuts.
Yummy scrummy."

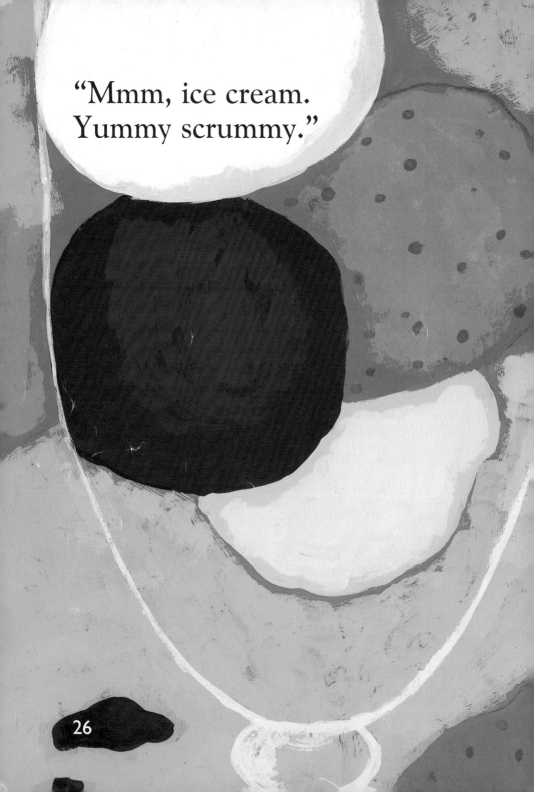

"Mmm, ice cream. Yummy scrummy."

26

THWAP!

28

"Yummy scrummy!"